The Simple Truth

*

a play in 14 scenes
(2019)

*

Traumear

List of Characters

GEORGE
NORMA, his wife

SUSAN (13) and TIM (9), their children

HENRY
PHILLIPA, wife of Henry

PAUL
FRED two acquaintances of George

CARLA friend of Fred

IRMA friend of Henry

JIMMY a Janitor

TWO SPIRITS (of family and of community)

*

The Simple Truth

1

PAUL visits GEORGE at home

Paul No, you're right, George, I'm not happy. Not content. I look it, do I? But what does that matter? Or put it this way: What business is it of yours? You're not even my friend. A mere acquaintance. Which means what? Nothing you can do for me. So why raise the subject. Let the subject lie. It lies in any case. It's a sleeping dog. I am going to have to look for work. No, I need money; what has work to do with it? I'd gladly work for nothing if I could find work that interested me. Work and money – two different issues, George. If I had a steady income I'd be perfectly at peace.

George Who wouldn't.

Paul Well, I disagree with you there too. Some people need to work to keep their juices flowing. They need to sweat, even intellectually sweat, and the reward is a temporary placidity of the bloodstream. Usually then somebody comes along and says: You have no right to work without pay! You are letting the side down! They force him to take money but he gives it away because all he wants to do is sweat. I believe they feel they have sinned and they need to make up for it. Oh strange delusion of mankind!

George They believe in a god. That's *their* problem. As soon as you believe in a god you have to appease him.

Paul	So what about you, George? You're a rich man. You float high above the petty concerns of the general population, don't you.
George	Oh? Is that so? Well, yes, I suppose I do, although …
Paul	Don't go on. Let's take it from there.
George	No, Paul, don't interrupt me in mid sentence. I do float, as you say, but for good reason. I float because I can swim. My family keeps me afloat. My work keeps me afloat. My philosophy of life too. It's all of the one piece, and I don't apologize for it. I'm a reasonable citizen with my feet on the ground and I support my favourite football team. You may make fun of that if you like but it all adds up.
Paul	I don't. I don't make fun of it. Good grief! Play your games. You have a perfect right. The world spins and perfect rights fly off on all sides. I, meanwhile, have a perfect right to wait. But I can see I'm wasting my time here.
George	Oh dear! What were you hoping to gain?
Paul	Nothing. Nothing. Say hello to Irma.
George	Norma?
Paul	Whatever. Yes, of course, Norma. Cheers!
	(Paul leaves)
George	Here, your bag? Too late. Wonder what's in it.
	Groceries. I'll take them home. What a character!

———

GEORGE, NORMA, the FAMILY SPIRIT
at George and Norma's home

Norma	If he keeps going like that he'll end in jail.
George	Would he mind?
Norma	Maybe not. But it does depress me that somebody like that exists – in our environment. Not that he's a member of our society, George, I know that. You're not friends with him, are you? Because that would obligate you, wouldn't it.
George	No, we're not friends, Norma. Don't you worry now. I've always made sure that we didn't become friends. Whenever there was risk of affection I steered clear.
Norma	We have to protect what we have, George, or we lose it. We worked hard for it. I wouldn't thank you for jeopardizing what we've achieved.
George	Remind me what that is, quickly?
Norma	I shouldn't have to. Or are you joking?
George	It's your attitude, Norma. It's a grasping attitude. I hate it.
Norma	If the woman doesn't grasp, the man fritters it away. That's the way it is.
George	I wonder now, do we teach our children to grasp?
Norma	You tell me. Wouldn't you say that at nine and thirteen they pick up what they need from us? Not everything has to be put in words. They will learn the value of property when they see how you and I value our property. I don't even want to talk about it, it's so obvious.

George	Anyway, I'm off to the gym. What time is dinner?
Norma	Today you look after yourself. I pick up the children from school and take them for a picnic. You're not invited because you were such a grouch last time.
George	What? Excuse me, Norma, are you in your right mind? You don't do that. You don't behave like that. What will Susan and Timmy think?
Norma	They will think what I tell them to think, George: I am punishing Daddy because last time he was a grouch. That way they will learn that being a grouch has con-sequences. They will learn either to be happy or else to pretend to be happy. Don't forget that these early lessons are character-forming.
George	How do you propose to pick up the children?
Norma	In the car. You are taking the bus to the gym.
George	Well, that's where you're wrong, dear. Actually I'm driving to the gym. Why? Because I want to. And because I had intended to. You are going to have to learn that lack of consideration has consequences. (*George leaves*)
Norma	George! Do as you're told! Damn it! I'm trying to teach the children how to obey! There he goes, doing as he pleases, as usual. Leaving me to look after the family. I'm going to have to figure something out. This can't go on. It's his will against mine, and mine is stronger.
The Family Spirit	(*appears*)
	Oh my, now look what a mistake you are making, dear! Let the family spirit point out to you a few of the benefits of love and affection. Without them there is …

4

Norma	Out! Out of my way! Out of my sight! Never presume to tell me what to do! If I don't hold this family together, against all comers, what will happen? I'll end in the poorhouse; and that's not a manner of speaking.
The Family Spirit	I certainly have no intention to undermine your authority over this household. You and you husband have …
Norma	No! I won't listen to you. You sow doubt. You are trying to confuse me. Just go back to where you came from. I want my world to be clear, logical, predictable and under control. To that end I wield my authority.
The Family Spirit	*(fades and disappears)*
Norma	There. I don't know what happened to me there. It has happened a few times since that first time about a year ago. On my birthday. Onsets of doubt. You have to fight them off. Oh heavens, the children! And no car! Now what? A taxi. So much for the picnic. Damn!

———

3

NORMA and PHILLIPA, later the COMMUNAL SPIRIT, at Norma's home

NORMA	No, Phillipa dear, no, he won't do what I say anymore. Love, honour and obey. Obey! Also I've had these mini blackouts. Always when I'm by myself. I come out of it and imagine I've been shouting at somebody.
PHILLIPA	That's peculiar. You, shouting? Have you been to a doctor about it?
NORMA	Don't be a smartass. He sent me to a psychiatrist. I told him what I thought of that. He must have thought

5

I was going crazy. I'm not there yet but the way
things are going – well, it wouldn't surprise me. And
it'll be George's fault.

PHILLIPA   Well, cheer up. You'll have that to hold over him then.

NORMA   It'll be something. It's an eternal competition, isn't it.
What about your Henry? Is he still playing around
with that dame in the sweeties shop?

PHILLIPA   He's not playing around with her, dear. He has honour-
able intentions. He told me so and I believe him. Why
would I not believe my own husband? Besides, when
was the last time you spoke to Henry? More than two
years ago. Because he said you were a bit judgemental
now and again. You're still holding that against him.
Even though he was right.

NORMA   What has right to do with it? You don't say that to a
woman. He forgot his place, that's all and I'm still
waiting for an apology.

PHILLIPA   You may wait, dear. He's not into apologies. I'm
waiting for a few myself. What are men not like!

THE COMMUNAL *SPIRIT*   *(appears)*
And then one day this human being discovered that
what comes out of your mouth can hurt you. Can
severely damage you. You two are paying no attention
to that at all. You might think about that if you have a
minute – in the name of communal spirit.

NORMA   Gracious me it's hot in here. Could we open a window?

PHILLIPA   Could we open a window indeed! Grateful I am to you
for that suggestion, dear. Could we let in some air.

THE COMMUNAL SPIRIT
It's all the same what you say to each other. Ever and
always the same.

6

NORMA   Am I being a bore or can you hear a voice like from outer space telling us to do this and that?

PHILLIPA   Space travel has never interested me but what you say draws after it a kind of echo effect, a sonar image, a boink it used to be called, in the outback; I should never have left.

THE COMMUNAL SPIRIT
    Keep in mind that communal spirit never further away than a stone's throw; in short than the stone you are about to throw. Oh what opportunities you have! As for me, I'm always looking for another home. So be careful now, because if you ignore me ...

NORMA   Did I screech loudly there, Phillipa? I thought I heard myself scream.

PHILLIPA   Yes you did. You did. Why did you scream? Is something hurting you? Did you recall the time when you committed an evil deed?

NORMA   I have never committed an evil deed in my life. I know nothing about evil. Watch your mouth! That sort of question is liable to get a person into trouble.

PHILLIPA   What kind of trouble, dear? I mean is it trouble I wouldn't be able to handle?

NORMA   How do you fancy being up in court? Can you see yourself answering questions such as: Where were you when the shit hit the fan? Why didn't you phone the police when you saw the assailant advancing with a sharp kitchen knife? They will look into your past and discover every sexual misdemeanour, every tax evasion, ever insult to the flag. Your own children will testify against you. Your husband will sell you down the river.

7

PHILLIPA   Norma! Why are you so horrid to me? What have I done to you to deserve this treatment?

NORMA   Simple. You accused me of evil. Did you forget that?

PHILLIPA   I meant that only in a sort of a way, for heaven's sake! Besides we're all evil, deep down. You're not alone.

(NORMA flings herself at her, manages to floor her and runs 'for a kitchen knife'. Phillipa escapes from the house)

NORMA   Lucky old Phillipa. (shouts after her) You won't get away next time! – That bitch. Oh I don't know, I should have moved faster. I'm losing my touch.

THE COMMUNAL SPIRIT   *(disappears)*

NORMA   – – My head! – – Oh no, look at the time! The Youngsters!   *(she runs off)*

———

4

GEORGE, SUSAN, TIM, FRED, later the FAMILY SPIRIT – at the gym

SUSAN   How come it was you who picked us up? Today was Mom's turn. What's up?

GEORGE   Big struggle, Susan. Struggle to the death, as usual. But never mind, we're here to enjoy ourselves.

TIM   At the gym? Since when?

GEORGE   Well, that's the way it is today. Timmy. Don't question it and you'll be alright. The more you question, the more lies you end up with; surely you've learned that by now.

SUSAN	No, honestly, what do you think I'm going to do here for an hour …
GEORGE	Two hours …
SUSAN	Two hours! While you pump yourself full of testosterone? I don't go for that at all. We can make it home by ourselves. Obviously we're caught up in the fight between you two again.
FRED	(arrives)
	Hija George. Hello kids. I've got a new deal for you, old buddy. Ten percent down, four hundred a month. You've been waiting for this one. This guy needs to bring home the bacon tout suite. Wife left him. He's near the edge. Up to you to take advantage. I take five percent, between friends. What do you say?
GEORGE	I'll look into it, Freddy, if you take these youngsters off my hands for a couple of hours. Show them the town. Come back here at six. Then we'll all go for dinner somewhere. A deal for a deal.
SUSAN	Oh for Christ's sake, I can't stand this guy. He wrecked my computer. Look, we can go home by ourselves.
GEORGE	You're too young to be by yourselves on the streets. I'd go to jail if I let you two out to play in the big city. And you wouldn't go straight home, would you. You might say you would but then you'd do as you please.
FRED	If they don't obey you, why would they obey me? Timmy, you like me, don't you? We got along alright last week. Or we would have, if your mother hadn't pitched into me and I lost my temper.
SUSAN	I don't know what liking has to do with it. *(she takes Tim aside, whispers to him, then returns to Fred)*

9

That's alright then, we'll come with you. Anything to get out of this smelly place. Come on, let's go.

GEORGE   You two do what you're told now, do you hear? Your mother is on the warpath. If you're home late she'll kill you. Thanks Freddy. Phone me.

FRED   Come on, kiddies. We'll have us a great time. And what Mommy and Daddy don't know won't hurt them.
            (*FRED exits with the children*)

THE FAMILY SPIRIT *enters.*
            This is so sad, George. On account of your behaviour, right now especially, your youngest child is going to die on the street and you might not even blame yourself for it. Run after them and take them home yourself in the car. Do it in the name of family spirit.

GEORGE   I'm not superstitious. I'm doing my best here.

THE FAMILY SPIRIT
            No you're not. All your thought is about your own convenience. As for love …

GEORGE   Don't … stop it! … Don't talk to me about love. It's a Christmas present for Fido the dog. I was in love once, for a short time, and instead of leaving it like that I made the horrendous mistake of marrying the girl.

THE FAMILY SPIRIT
            It was not a mistake, George. The mistake all along has been that you didn't bother learning how to love.

GEORGE   Do you know what? Even that word I hate. It makes me feel sick, I can tell *you* that. It's an illusion and sex destroys it. Not that I don't know the odd couple who get along. But what sort of pious lives do they lead? I always suspect that they're nice to each other so as to deserve the afterlife – however they picture that, ac-

10

cording to their church dogma. How can you respect love if it doesn't turn you into a proper human being? That's what I'd like to be some day, a proper, bona fide human being, with at least a smidgen of self-respect, maybe a sense of honour, of self-worth. But that will never happen.

THE FAMILY SPIRIT

Why can it not happen?

GEORGE   Because I'm too god-damned tangled up in this excuse of a family life. I can't think for myself, I'm that worried somebody will know what I'm thinking.

THE FAMILY SPIRIT

Let me make you a bargain, George. When I leave here you'll wonder where you've been for the last ten minutes. I can do that for you. It's not much, but it will help you remember what we've talked about. It will be like a key for you. Now to make it worthwhile you will have to agree to a short extension to this conversation. So far it was *my* idea. If you agree to the extension, that part will be your idea and then that will be what you remember. What do you say?

GEORGE   I say go ahead, what have I got to lose.

THE FAMILY SPIRIT

That's the spirit! Now I want you to think back to the time when you were three and a half years old. I'll jog your memory. Your mother had left you on your own for a minute. You toddled across the street to a bridge over a stream. You looked down into the water and became fascinated. Do you recall that now?

GEORGE   I do, actually.

THE FAMILY SPIRIT
As you gazed into the water you dreamt a little dream. I was in that dream. There was some danger that you'd get caught up in it. So I allowed you to fall into the water. Your mother heard you and pulled you out. Of course I knew she would. You were perfectly alright. And you had that little dream inside you. It's been ripening there like a plum on a tree. The time you have existed since then will seem to you like death warmed up when you look back on it from where you will find yourself if you take my advice.

GEORGE
Sure it seems like death warmed up right now. So go ahead, advise me.

THE FAMILY SPIRIT
Good for you. (*the spirit leaves*)

GEORGE
I'm daydreaming again. Look at me, one sock on and one sock off. I feel burdened. Maybe it's a good burden. Actually I don't want to continue here at all now. You'd think I was doing all this to spite Norma. (*He gets ready to go.*)

———

5

HENRY, IRMA at Irma's place

IRMA
So is Phillipa getting suspicious, Henry?

HENRY
Suspicious of what? God, Irma, why are you always trying to get something going? She knows we have a relationship, I've told you that before.

IRMA
Ah yes, of course. Good old Phillipa. I'd like to explain a few things to her. I do think I'll call her up.

HENRY	Pay her a visit, why don't you. So far she was just happy knowing you were there. My Henry has a female friend.
IRMA	How come she never gets a friend for herself? No imagination?
HENRY	She has plenty of friends. Some of them are *our* friends.
IRMA	Does she indeed! I must look into that. Find out what's going on.
HENRY	Be my guest, Irma. You spend too much time in your little shop. You have such a good heart. Take a little interest in what's going on around you. It's not healthy, the way you live. Actually I think that's why I come to see you. I'm interested in your welfare. I should like you to develop your mind, my dear.
IRMA	What! Read Schopenhauer and listen to Beethoven? No thanks.
HENRY	I wouldn't have thought you'd even know those names. However did you come across them?
IRMA	I used to take courses. When *I* tried to improve myself. You can tell it didn't do me much good. By the way, the youngster that was killed in the traffic yesterday. I recognized the name. Your friend George's son.
HENRY	No! Not Timmy! Oh I'm so sorry. He was a nice wee chap. He and his sister Susan used to lock themselves into the toilet when George and Irma were fighting. Ach, that's a shame, isn't it?
IRMA	Why? Because he was a child? Rather a child than a mature adult, that's what I always say. Far too many

13

children around. What are they good for? Very few mature adults.

HENRY   Oh God, Irma, the stuff you come up with! I hope you never have children.

IRMA   I'd not let them run into the traffic.

HENRY   It happens, doesn't it.

IRMA   It happens more to some than to others. George Proctor is a businessman, isn't he? From what I read in the papers, he doesn't much care where his money comes from.

HENRY   True enough, he's not a paragon of virtue. But who is?

IRMA   Shall we keep in mind degrees, dearest?

HENRY   Yes, of course.

IRMA   Anyway, it's one less annoyance for him now.

HENRY   I must send my condolences.

IRMA   You do that. Meanwhile young Timmy is out of it and I'm glad.

HENRY   You've never met those children, have you?

IRMA   They've been in and out of this shop many a time. They used to sit with me in the back, Henry, and complain about their parents. They said home was hell. I used to advise them to keep a low profile. They were afraid their parents were going to kill each other one day and where would that leave them. Imagine! They were not even teenagers yet, when fears like that were planted into them.

HENRY   I see you don't just sell sweets here.

IRMA	I know George and Norma Proctor through the mouths of their children. And don't you imagine that I persuaded them to talk. I didn't have to. They mitched whole afternoons sometimes. Their teachers were afraid to talk to Norma.
HENRY	I can imagine that. Oh dear! I have to be going, Irma. I do love our little tête-à-têtes.
IRMA	As long as that's all they are.
HENRY	I can't imagine how they could be more. I'm a better husband for having you as a friend.
IRMA	Well, keep up the good work. I understand that Phillipa is toying with the notion of going into politics.
HENRY	She's not just toying, Irma. She's very unhappy with the state of this country. I tell her it's all due to a healthy transition and she says she wants to be part of the transition, you know, steer it in the right direction. I ask what's the right way? how can we know? and she replies: Some know and some don't.
IRMA	Do you wish her well?
HENRY	Of course I do. And she's raised a bundle of money already.
IRMA	Has she? Good for her. Look will you give her this, to put *to* it, and tell here I'll work for her if she wants. I have some experience.
HENRY	Oh Irma! Can you afford all that?
IRMA	At the moment, yes. I know what she's after and I sympathize.
HENRY	Well, thank you. See you soon, eh?

IRMA   Surely.

———

6

PAUL and JIMMY in Paul's flat,

PAUL   What I want to do – what I want to be known to be
            doing – how I can do it without making a fool of
            myself – all these are the sort of questions a thoroughly
            modern man asks himself while he's having a drink by
            himself on a night when sleep will not come because it
            can't be bothered – or because it lacks respect for the
            guy who wishes he could forget for a few hours that
            he's a failure in more ways than one … why is the
            night, the time when we're most exposed, also the time
            when the gremlins come out to cheapen the soul …
            soul? Stupid question. Besides … what soul … just a
            black hole where nothing grows because everything
            dies in it. An astronomic projection.
            (he telephones)
            Hello, Jimmy? Paul here. I'll give you fifty bucks if
            you get out of the sack and come up here to the pent-
            house. I need to talk to somebody or I'm going to
            jump. You will? Bless you for a good janitor.
            (hangs up)
            Now there's a man with a heart of gold. A man with a
            philosophy. His wife died of cancer last year. His only
            son has been sectioned. Here he's willing to leave his
            bed at three-thirty in the morning for fifty bucks –
            which he won't even accept, if I know him. Why can't
            I be like that? Where have I gone wrong? We're born
            all the same, aren't we? We begin to differ on this

16

side of the womb. It's all about nurture and growth, isn't it? Or is it?
(knock at the door)
Come in, Jimmy!

JIMMY   *(enters, takes a long look at Paul)*
Yes sir, Mr. Paul, you have the long face. You have those bags under the eyes that tell me you have the weight of the world on your shoulders. Fifty bucks to set you straight? Make it a hundred.

PAUL   Name your price, Jimmy. We've had the odd talk and every time afterwards I respect myself a little.

JIMMY   That's because I respect *you*, Mr. Paul. You are a good man but you don't believe it. You have to learn how to believe.

PAUL   Nonsense. No such thing as a good man. You're not a good man either, Jimmy, but you have character. Where did you get it?

JIMMY   You're right, Mr. Paul. I have character. Where did I get it? I rolled with the punches and I soaked up the pain. I made my own music until they broke my fiddle. Then I sang for a while. Today all I can do is hum. But I hum my own tune. And those angels in heaven are jealous because they can't even hum.

PAUL   Do you want a drink, Jimmy? *(pours himself a glass)* I know, you don't drink. How do you manage to forget? I know, you have no reason to forget. Me, I need to drink. But now, because you're here, I'm not going to drink either. *(pushes his glass away)* You see what's wrong, don't you. Nobody depends on me. No wife, no children, no friends. And why is that? Because I push everybody away. As soon as they get friendly I push them away. And don't tell me to stop doing that

	because that's me. I am the way I behave. For some reason. Now tell me why I behave like that, Jimmy.
JIMMY	Nothing simpler, Mr. Paul. You push everyone away because you don't want them to interfere with what you would be doing if you knew what to do. So I tell you what to do, no? I tell you now, and maybe you listen and maybe you hear?
PAUL	Go ahead, Jimmy. I'm all ears.
JIMMY	You look inside yourself, that's what you do now. That's where the fear is and that's where you look, Mr. Paul. Are you doing that now?
PAUL	Tell me more.
JIMMY	Now you believe what you see. The same way you believe that you sit on that chair and that your name is Mr. Paul, you believe what you see. Don't you look at what you see, but you believe it. You believe whatever you see. Keep at it. It takes practice. Believe what you see when you look inside yourself. Because that's where it is what you need, when you look and you see and believe. Jimmy knows what he's talking about. And don't you take any argument from anybody who tells you you should stop looking and seeing and believing inside yourself. The night is young. I go back downstairs now, so you don't see me for a little while. Then, in another little while, you will see me again because I'll be coming back, knocking on you door and you will say: Come in, Jimmy, I'm one hundred percent. Here I go now. (*JIMMY leaves*)

———

18

JIMMY in his penthouse,
then PAUL in Jimmy's flat

JIMMY

(on his knees)
Oh god, help that Mr Paul to see the light. You are the light and he thinks it's dark. I've reminded him of you but now you have to pinch him in the right place to wake him up. It's because I'm praying for him, that is why you are able to do that, I think I understand that right. He is like me in every way except that I know you and he doesn't. At least not yet. Or maybe by now he does. – I'm not going to continue to push my case here, as if you didn't understand what I mean or as if you were miles away and I needed to shout. That Mr. Paul needs to have you on his side, I know that. And so much the better for you if you have him on your side, right? There, that's all I'm going to say. Maybe you see reasons why this can't work. I've done my best.

(JIMMY goes to the door and there's a knock. He opens and there stands PAUL.)

PAUL

Jimmy, what's keeping you? Didn't you say you'd come back? I was sitting there waiting and waiting. As long as you're alright. Can I come in for a few minutes? I can tell you haven't been back to bed yet.

JIMMY

Of course you can, Mr. Paul. I will make us some coffee. Make yourself comfortable.

PAUL

Thank you. It's good to have a friend. I thought about what you said, by the way. And I did it for quite a while. Who can say, maybe it did me good, eh?

JIMMY	Of course it did you good. It's doing you good right now, Mr. Paul. I can tell. But you have to look within yourself now and again if you want to make a proper start. We're not on earth to sit and wait until the good god pushes our buttons.
PAUL	Oh, now, don't talk to me about God. That, to me, is a fairytale. When I was a youngster I had to go to church and I hated it.
JIMMY	Milk and sugar?
PAUL	Beg your pardon?
JIMMY	In your coffee. Milk and sugar?
PAUL	Oh yes. Plenty of sugar, Jimmy. I'm awake now and I intend to stay awake. Do you know what I thought I might do tomorrow? I will go for a long walk. Not for years have I been for a walk.
JIMMY	Where will you go, Mr. Paul?
PAUL	I don't know yet, Jimmy. I think I'll go wherever the spirit takes me.
JIMMY	What spirit is that, Mr. Paul?
PAUL	Oh that's just a saying, Jimmy. I shall take a step and then stop and ask myself: Do I turn left now, or right, or do I continue on straight? Then I will take the next step. Like that.
JIMMY	You will be making slow progress.
PAUL	Come to think of it, Jimmy, I don't want to make any progress at all, for a change. I want to sit tight while I walk. Does that make sense?
JIMMY	As long as you know where you sit while you walk.

PAUL	To be sure. That's good coffee. A real treat! Do you know what? I'm glad I called on you last night.
JIMMY	Oh, is it morning already, Mr. Paul?
PAUL	It feels like it to me, Jimmy. Isn't that strange! If it weren't still dark outside I'd start out on my walk right now.
JIMMY	(*looks out the window*) The sky is clear, Mr. Paul. If you set out now you will see the sun rise.
PAUL	Well, that would be the first time. – I say, why not! Why not start out right now!
JIMMY	Do that. Start out right now.
PAUL	By God I will. Imagine that now. I will go upstairs, I will get out my rucksack, put in some water, maybe a sandwich, a chocolate bar, I will wear my down-filled jacket because it's bound to be still cold – and I will walk. When I get to where I want to be I will either stay there or else turn around and come back. You might get a telephone call from Bessarabia, Jimmy. Hah! Here I go.
JIMMY	I look forward to that, Mr. Paul. I will keep an eye on your flat. (*they shake hands. **Paul** leaves. – **Jimmy** is seen to be getting down on his knees again.*)

———

8

NORMA and PAUL
(PAUL comes across NORMA in black on a park bench)

PAUL	Norma! Is that you? You don't look too happy. What's wrong?

21

NORMA	Don't talk to me.
PAUL	Why are you dressed in black? Is somebody dead?
NORMA	You are really the most insensitive bastard I have ever come across. What makes you think you can … you don't know that Tim is dead? My son Tim?
PAUL	I don't believe it! What happened? Norma, I'm sorry! That's terrible. Of course I didn't know. I haven't seen George in over a week. Please tell me. How did he die?
NORMA	You're the first person I've spoken to since we buried him who sounds as if he was really sorry. Paul, sit down with me for a little. I'm completely messed up inside. I've been blaming George and he blames me. We can't even talk to each other. Secretly I suspected something like this was going to happen. The door between George and me has been closed for a long time now. It was one constant struggle for supremacy. And our children? Well, just sometimes I seemed to notice, out of the corner of my eye, how much our fighting disturbed them but I didn't let it matter to me. I believe you could safely say that we both killed Timmy.
PAUL	Would it help you to talk about how it happened, Norma?
NORMA	George picked them up from school. I should have, it was my turn, but he … oh I have to stop blaming him! Anyway, he took Susan and Timmy with him to the gym and then he let Freddy Bingham take them home from there. What did *he* do? He lost control of them. No, they ran away. It's not his fault either. Then Timmy must have run in front of a car. I didn't even recognize him at the morgue, Paul. That's how badly

22

	he was injured. And Susan saw it, of course. She hasn't been able to speak for three days. It's a punishment come down from heaven.
PAUL	I'm so sorry. To lose a young child like that!
NORMA	He was my favourite. That's probably another reason why I lost him. Our priest explained it to me like that. Do you think he's right to say that?
PAUL	I would think that maybe if he had said a thing like that next year sometime ... but is that even a reasonable thing to say, Norma? And as for punishment from heaven ... what does that mean, exactly? I thought heaven was a merciful affair, is that not right? I was always told that it's we ourselves who do the punishing. I think you might suffer the pain as best you can and never worry about punishment. Pain is a doctor of sorts, if we put up with the treatment – gladly, if possible – .
NORMA	Is that right, Paul? How do you know that?
PAUL	I don't know how I know it. I have been having the most unusual thoughts since Monday. I've mostly been walking ... as far as the city ... and I'm just on my way back home. I think it's a good omen that I bumped into you, Norma. Let's not question it. So you were saying George is not coping too well either?
NORMA	George wanted to kill himself. He does blame himself but of course he doesn't admit it. We have to take a good look at our life together, George and I. No, I do think that's what this accident is about. Let's face it, Timmy isn't in any pain. He's out of it. Susan will need help of some sort, sooner of later. I don't think she trusts George and me at all. She'll be fourteen in June.

23

PAUL	Let's walk a bit, Norma, do you mind? Let's walk in that direction. You shouldn't be alone.
NORMA	Alright. This is very kind of you. Just don't come too close.

(they walk off together, talking)

9

PAUL and NORMA arrive at George and Norma's house

PAUL	Hello George.
GEORGE	Paul.
NORMA	You see what I mean? What did I tell you. He won't even greet me. As though I were to blame. Let me tell you something, my friend, we share this equally. I've been talking to Paul. He is head and shoulders above you when it comes to insight. You should listen to him.
GEORGE	It's difficult, Paul. Awkward, to say the least. I'm trying to take responsibility but all I come up with is this rage, as if I had to hide behind somebody else. It's enough for me to look at Norma and I find myself clenching my fists. I don't trust myself near her. She made me do it. That's what keeps going through my head. Do what? What did I do? Maybe it's what I didn't do. But how can I still blame anybody then? Maybe I should blame circumstances.
PAUL	You might as well blame the fact that you're born. That's when people commit suicide. It's their last resource.

24

GEORGE	I'm afraid some vindictive power is going to remove me from the earth, so I will beat him to it. That sort or thing? Can you really think, Paul? I never knew that.
PAUL	I am absolutely on your side, you two, if there is any side to take. If I had any children of my own I'd be tempted to feel something like: rather they than me; but I don't, so I can sense how this must be devastating for both of you – partly, I dare say, because you know that you've not been the best of parents, and what parents have been the best of parents, but also because your own flesh and blood has been cut off. A saint would say: God gives and god takes, but who can be a saint every hour of the day.
GEORGE	I hear what you say, but from a distance, Paul. All the same, don't think I'm not grateful. It's that Norma and I don't see eye to eye about anything. That's the worst.
NORMA	Timmy is pointing that out to us, isn't he.
GEORGE	There's Freddy now, he blames himself too. But he did his best and he probably knows it. We never did our best, Norma.
NORMA	Speak for yourself. I tried. Oh how I tried!
GEORGE	Well yes, I should speak for myself. I was vindictive. And it felt good, being vindictive. I felt righteous.
NORMA	Self-righteous, more like.
GEORGE	Why don't you ... ! Oh God help me, will it never end?
NORMA	You see? He wants to kill me. He will, one day.
GEORGE	It's not me, it's not me, Norma. It's this rage. It builds and it builds. How can a man live like that? Always wanting to hurt and harm somebody. Never really at

	peace. You know what I do at night? I don't sleep any more. I stare into space and my muscles fidget and jump, so that I have to hang on to myself for dear life or I get up and do something terrible.
NORMA	I don't want to be in the same house with him any more, Paul. You can see that, can't you.
PAUL	Actually that might be a good idea, if you two stay separate for a short while. My flat is big enough for two, George. Bunk in with me for a few days, a few weeks, if necessary.
NORMA	A good idea, Paul. Get him out of my sight for a while.
GEORGE	Would I still want to kill her while I'm staying with you?
PAUL	Go on. Let's do it right now. – I mean, while I have a chat with Norma you pack up some things in your suitcase.
NORMA	The car stays here. I need the car.
PAUL	Of course, Norma. Here's the key to my flat, George. Please. Don't think twice about it. When you're ready just call a taxi and go. Or let me know and I'll call a taxi.
NORMA	Sure he knows how to use his phone, doesn't he? Why are you mothering him?
PAUL	This is very hard for both of you. Right now he's bound to think of you as a black-hearted witch, Norma, and you can't help but imagine that you're in the right. But I'm at this moment blessed with being able to imagine the truth and that is why you two are smart to just go along with my suggestion.

(*GEORGE leaves*)

26

NORMA	As soon as he's out of the room I can relax.
PAUL	That's perfectly understandable. Here is my telephone number, Norma. I want you to call me if you want help with getting the groceries or if you just want to talk. I intend to stay with you for a few more minutes, to give George plenty of time to sort himself out.
NORMA	Remind him to take his toothbrush, would you? He has a special brush because of …Oh yes, and some of his socks are in the wash. – But he can buy more, can't he? (*she weeps wretchedly while Paul consoles her. Suddenly SUSAN stands there and asks:*)
SUSAN	What's going on? (*NORMA opens her arms towards her and SUSAN walks off*)
NORMA	That's just right. She realizes I'm feeling sorry for myself. I'm going to have to let somebody else do that for me. At least she spoke. She hasn't spoken since …
PAUL	I know; you told me.
NORMA	Are you sure it's alright if I call you when I'm stuck?
PAUL	Let's behave like human beings, Norma. It will do me good. It's the weekend, so Susan is off school. Has she been going to school?
NORMA	Paul, I have no idea what she's been doing. We walk past each other like strangers these days. I'm beginning to realize the full horror of that.
PAUL	I guess that's progress. That's the taxi I hear now. It's moving off. Where's my rucksack? I'm going to walk home. I've been walking for three days. I told you that in the park, didn't I. Good. Let's leave it

27

like that for the moment. What a blessing that we have telephones.

(PAUL offers to shake hands and NORMA accepts. PAUL leaves)

———

10

FRED, CARLA
(in CARLA'S flat)

FRED   Come sit with me here for a minute, Carla. Stop fussing about. We're only just up and you have half a day's work done.

CARLA   And what's wrong with that, Freddy? Work is my pleasure.

FRED   Really? That's interesting. How long do we know each other now?

CARLA   A day and a night, Freddy. It's our first date. And you remembered my name, that's nice.

FRED   The whole idea of going on a date is to learn a new name. Imagine you spending the night with me too. Well well.

CARLA   Actually you spent it with me, eh? But I trust you, Freddy. When I trust somebody I don't mind letting them know.

FRED   A whole lot goes on in your mind; I've noticed that. You are so different from me – you know, the way you think, your tastes, what upsets you and what doesn't – that, to my mind, makes it worth my while

28

	to get to know you. And you don't try to please me – at least I don't get that impression. Do you?
CARLA	Try to please you? Maybe if it happens. It's nice being with somebody who has no hang-ups. Ouch. I've cut myself. Have you … Oh I have one in my bag. A plaster. Maybe you can get it out for me so that I don't get … in that side pocket. Got it. Just wrap it round tight. Fine. Quick, the pancakes are burning. No, you just sit down now and pour us both some coffee. Delightful!
FRED	What's delightful?
CARLA	Oh this entire scene. You in your dressing gown, the table set nicely for two and it's the start of a new day. Isn't it great to be alive?
FRED	Come to think of it, yes.
CARLA	But you're preoccupied. I can tell. What's bothering you, Freddy? Tell you friend Carla.
FRED	What's bothering me? Well, you might as well know. I agreed to be responsible for a couple of children and one of them ran into the traffic.
CARLA	On no! Dead?
FRED	Dead alright. A nine year old boy. Headstrong chap. Wouldn't do what I told him. Stay by my side, I said. I should have expected as much. He had no upbringing. Wasn't used to obedience, know what I mean? Still, it shook me up.
CARLA	You have to make that work for you now.
FRED	How do you mean?

CARLA	Well, evidently it's bothering you. You feel responsible, don't you? Own it. Take possession of it. Make it part of you.
FRED	Carla, whatever are you talking about?
CARLA	I can see you need to be educated. When you've messed up you have to learn from it. Assume the responsibility. Tell me if I'm coming on too strong for you.
FRED	No, it's not that. But I have to think now. This is new territory for me. You mean that lump in my chest is meant to do me good?
CARLA	I couldn't have put it better myself. Take another pancake. Here's butter. Here's syrup. Use it. It's free. I have often had a lump in my chest like that. It's because I trust people and when they don't trust back I feel like I've misled them. Big lump.
FRED	Now tell me in detail, not in big words, Carla, how I should rid myself of the painful knowledge that I've caused pain. Can you do that for me? I've been negligent and caused pain.
CARLA	You consider yourself to be a human being, don't you?
FRED	I suppose I do that, yes.
CARLA	Which means that you either get bigger and better or smaller and worse, is that not so?
FRED	I've never thought of it but I guess you're right.
CARLA	So let's assume that you want to get bigger and better.
FRED	Fair enough, Socrates.

CARLA	Hahaha! And would you say you get bigger and better by assuming the responsibility for your mistakes or by denying it and blaming people and circumstances?
FRED	Oh, the latter, Socrates.
CARLA	So what about the pain?
FRED	I won't worry about it. I ... ah ... I have better things to do.
CARLA	Such as?
FRED	Oh dear, let me thing ... I'm going to love the people I've hurt?
CARLA	Oh that's good! I never thought of that. Anything else?
FRED	I'll talk it over with them and I will let them blame me if they want to but that won't worry me because I'm already admitting fault. I will confess my liability and ask them if there is anything I can do to make restitution.
CARLA	Oh Freddy! You are talking like a proper human being now. Can I be your friend?
FRED	Anybody would want Socrates for a friend.
CARLA	Well, that's great then. I look forward to this friendship.
FRED	Do you want to go for a walk? The sun is shining.
CARLA	Oh good, let's do that! Just you and me. Two human beings going for a walk in the sunshine. How good is that, eh? First I'm going to stack these few dishes. Meanwhile you ...
FRED	Yes indeed. I get dressed. Things are looking up for me. We've made a bit of sense, haven't we?

———

31

11

NORMA and PHILLIPA, later IRMA,
at Norma's house

NORMA   No. Paul! That is the name of the young man he left
with. Try to get this straight, Phillipa. He's gone. You
should have seen me.

PHILLIPA   Who is this Paul? I haven't heard of him. What's his
last name?

NORMA   Oh it doesn't matter. I don't know. A business
colleague of George's. A crafty lad, if you ask me.

PHILLIPA   Well yes, I do ask you, Norma. Make up your mind.
Are you glad you are rid of George or are you heart-
broken that he's gone?

NORMA   I can't make up my mind. There. Will that do you?
You ask the stupidest questions.

PHILLIPA   Norma, if you get nasty again I leave immediately.
You practically beat me up last time. What were you
going to get from the kitchen? A knife maybe? It's
just possible that you are not safe to be around. And
for all I know, neither is George.

NORMA   Where is Susan? What have you done with her? Is it
not enough that I've lost my Timmy? Now you take
Susan away? What kind of a friend are you?

PHILLIPA   But I told you. She met Henry and came with him to
our place. She doesn't want to go home. She says you
make her sick. (*NORMA makes as if to attack
Phillipa*) Look here. Do you know what this is? It's a
pistol. If you attack me I'm going to blow your brains
out. Is that understood?

NORMA   You damned well wouldn't!

PHILLIPA   I don't think I would either, Norma, but if you push
            me enough, I will lose my own head this time. So by
            God, I might. I think there's something a little wrong
            with your brain. A few brain cells are unhinged;
            temporarily, I hope. Stop there! My finger is on the
            trigger, Norma. Somebody has to tell you this. Susan
            will not set foot in this house for the foreseeable
            future. She is strangely mature for her age and she
            knows what she wants and how to get it. She also
            knows what she doesn't want, and that is anything to
            do with you or George. Pretend you have no children.

NORMA   Can I go into the kitchen?

PHILLIPA   No you can't. Not for the moment. You probably have
            a gun in the kitchen. I'm going to tell you a few more
            home truths, at gun point. If I describe in a courtroom
            how you have behaved recently, and also on previous
            occasions to George, you will be locked away. Also
            Susan will be taken away from you. In your present
            state you are incapable of thinking like a parent.

NORMA   How dare you! How dare you!

PHILLIPA   Sit down! This is the simple truth I'm telling you,
            because you're my friend. Never before in my life
            have I told anyone the simple truth; I want you to
            know that. In some perverted sense I'm even grateful
            to you for making that happen. So we're done being
            social for the moment. But that does not mean we
            need to stop being friends. You are a curse to yourself
            and this is my last attempt to get through to you.
                            (doorbell)

PHILLIPA   I will get this. You sit tight.
                    (opens door, lets IRMA in)

33

Ah, good. Now listen to this, Norma. This is Irma, Henry's friend from the sweetie shop. Don't smirk, you haven't a clue. While I was still at home she paid George and me a visit, as friends do. I told her I had decided to come over here and I let her in on a few secrets that explain you and George. She felt you must be having an awful time and immediately suggested she come with me. I asked her to wait until later because you are becoming more and more unpredictable. Irma is convinced it's grief. Not for Timmy but for your marriage and for your life in general. So here she is now and I want you to welcome her to your house, like a grown-up. Will you do that?

NORMA Irma, is it? Listen, Irma. She has been pointing a gun at me. Am I supposed to be able to speak normally to you?

PHILLIPA I have put the pistol away, as you can see, Norma.

NORMA Alright. Have a seat there, Irma. At the moment I am suffering a mental paralysis. I have been shouted at and I have been threatened with a gun and I have kept my nerve. When I look at you close up now I get the impression that you are a good woman. By good I mean good intentions. Do you think I could be helped?

IRMA Oh Norma! You *are* having an awful time. (*rushes to her to sit beside her on the settee and takes her hand in her own*) Of course you can be helped. Everybody can be helped. We all need one another's help. That's why we're alive. (*NORMA stares at her*) What would you rally like to change about your life if you had the choice?

34

NORMA	Nobody has ever asked me that question. What I'd like to change is the way I always think I'm the only one who knows. Everybody else is waiting for me to sort out the world for them and if I don't do it *(tears, nearly)* if I don't do it, my own world will fall apart. I don't mean to boss people about. I just want to tell them what's right and then they should do it. Is that not reasonable?
IRMA	And that goes for your husband and your children too?
NORMA	Most of all for them.
IRMA	Oh Norma, that is such a heavy burden you are placing on yourself.
NORMA	It's the way I was brought up, Irma. I don't know any other way. When somebody accuses me of anything my mind flips. All I can think is: How dare they accuse me when they're so much worse.
IRMA	Well, you're quite right to think that, Norma. We should never accuse one another.
NORMA	There! What did I say, Phillipa! Was I right or not? But you point a gun at me and tell me I'm deranged. What kind of a friend is that!
IRMA	Tell you what, Norma. Would you like to go for a little holiday with me, maybe for a week or two. I have already booked a flight for me to Crete next Friday. It would make me ever so happy to have you for company. Phillipa, you and Henry are glad to look after Susan for a while, am I right?
PHILLIPA	Certainly, if that's alright with Norma.
IRMA	And your husband is staying with a friend too, for the time being?

NORMA	He is, yes. So I could come with you. I feel like a youngster being invited to go on a school outing. Would this house still be here if I locked it up and went away and came back in a week's time?
PHILLIPA	I would keep an eye on it for you, Norma. *(NORMA has a good cry at this stage and PHILLIPA brings her a box of tissues)*
IRMA	Come with me right now, Norma. We will get a bite to eat somewhere, I'm hungry. Then I will show you where I live and you can watch me book another seat on that same plane to Heraklion. The sooner I do that the better. Then we will come back here and pick up what you need for staying with me till Friday and what you want to take with you to Crete. We'll have great time, wait till you see. *(NORMA gives her a hug)*
PHILLIPA	As for me, Norma, I will go home now and make some dinner for Henry and Susan and me. Have you a message for your daughter?
NORMA	No. No. Not now. Take good care of her, won't you?
PHILLIPA	Surely. *(IRMA and NORMA leave after IRMA gives PHILLIPA a hug and whispers "thank you" in her ear)*

12

(SUSAN, PHILLIPA and HENRY
at Phillipa and Henry's house)

PHILLIPA	And you are not to worry about your mother, Susan. She is perfectly …
SUSAN	I don't worry about my mother.

36

HENRY	Leave her alone now. Leave the child alone. She knows she can come and go as she pleases and we trust her completely. That's the best we can do.
PHILLIPA	Will you in fact do the best you can do, Susan? Or will you get into bad company and start using drugs?
SUSAN	Maybe. If that's the best I can do.
PHILLIPA	It's most annoying the way you talk in .., well, in statements. You strike me as someone who is full of hate.
HENRY	Good grief, Phillipa!
PHILLIPA	I'm making conversation. Young people really have no conversation. It has to be learned. I say something. Then you say something predictable that fits in with what I said. Then I say something predictable that fits in with what you said. What's so difficult about that? It's the only way to avoid this creeping depression. The young are suffering from creeping depression. Let's practice this a bit more, Susan. If I say: 'My belly hurts, I think I may be pregnant,' what might you say?
SUSAN	Take your fucking bellyache and shove it up your arse?
PHILLIPA	Well, that's creative. It's also rude. Could you say the same thing, essentially, but avoiding rude words?
SUSAN	Why are you so short of understanding? Why can you not understand that where I come from you have no jurisdiction? Every word I use sounds like a word you use but means something entirely different. You and I cannot converse.
PHILLIPA	Well, I don't know now, I understood perfectly what you said there. I don't believe it but I understood it. All that remains for me now is to prove to you that you're wrong and I'm right. I'm the adult, I trail

37

clouds of experience, my dear, and you, a mere slip of a thing, should listen and learn. This generation gap can be bridged. I wish you would say something, Henry.

HENRY   There's lack of mutual respect. I'm a man in my early forties and I feel like the world is a madhouse and life is passing me by.

PHILLIPA   Oh, that's great. Susan will learn a lot from you then, won't she. I can only wonder what it was that has brought on this sudden confession.

HENRY   Why is it that you are starting to sound like Norma? It's frightening.

SUSAN   Can I go out now?

HENRY   Of course you can, Susan. You don't have to ask.

PHILLIPA   Wait a mo. Are you mad? Susan is a minor. We are responsible for this child. For her safety. For her well-being. Under the law. Before she goes anywhere I want to know where she goes and when she will be back. That is how parents behave. At least they should.

SUSAN   But look, I can tell you a parcel of lies and you can do nothing about it. I can tell you I am going to a friend's house and will be back at six. Then I go for a walk in the woods and come back at nine. What can you do about it?

HENRY   Perfectly right, Susan. So far as I'm concerned you have the wisdom of a child. In addition to that, god takes care of children. Grown-ups only interfere. All the bad things teenagers do are reactions to ignorant grownups. It's immature adults who are to blame for the grief of children. There, you wanted me to speak, Phillipa, and I've spoken.

PHILLIPA   Yes, and look at Susan, she is sitting there smirking.

SUSAN   No, you're wrong. I'm not smirking. I'm happy.

PHILLIPA   Yes, at my expense. Oh, I don't know. Are you and I immature adults, Henry?

HENRY   Well, yes we are. Let's face it, we have no natural authority. I imagine that if I were mature I would automatically elicit respect. Instead, after I've spoken I invariably wish I hadn't.

PHILLIPA   Yes, there is this lingering soul-sickness, isn't there. The underlying suspicion that we're actually deaf and blind.
(SUSAN quietly leaves the room)
I strongly feel that I ought to go back to the beginning and start again. Maybe study the map more carefully this time.

HENRY   Do you suppose Norma and Irma are getting on in Crete?

PHILLIPA   Are you feeling nostalgic about Irma again?

HENRY   Well, she has it, hasn't she. She has what you and I are missing. To think that only the other day I felt superior to her.

PHILLIPA   People's character continually changes.

HENRY   The same goes for us too then, right?

PHILLIPA   We have judgmental minds and empty bodies.

HENRY   Not always, dear. Not always. There's hope for us. – – By the way, where is Susan?

PHILLIPA   Oh for heaven's sake! One minute she was here and the next minute she's gone. – Do you think maybe we only imagined her?

HENRY   She'll be alright, don't you worry. In a way she's more mature than we are. Let's stay in the background and maybe just shout before she falls into a hole or off a balcony.

13

(GEORGE and PAUL, then FRED and CARLA – at Paul's flat)

PAUL   No no, George, its not a problem, on the contrary. You are able to spend some time on your own while I'm away during the day and in the evening we compare notes. Now that I'm working for a living I have to rethink my philosophy, so I'm glad to have you to talk to.

GEORGE   That happened very quickly didn't, you taking an interest in work.

PAUL   Well, I told you about the chat I had with Jimmy the janitor. He pointed something out to me. – Yes, he sure did. –

GEORGE   You said he caused you to reflect?

PAUL   Yes, certainly that. Something crucial budged in me, that's for sure. I have no idea what it was but from one day to the next I realized that I was not meant to continue to vegetate. I told you I went for a walk. I was on the road for three days and nights. I slept rough, in a field once. On the second night a complete stranger took me in. During the third night I never put my head down and in the following morning I bumped into this woman I told you about. A business woman with an interest in music. I told her I had composed a bit, mostly for the piano and she literally put me to work the next day.

GEORGE And you are both going to the same teacher, you said?

PAUL I had no idea there was so much work available for budding composers. There's the phone. I'll take it next door.
(PAUL leaves and returns shortly afterwards)
Well, how about that! That was somebody who said he'd heard you were staying with me. He wants to come around for an hour with his friend. I say fine. What do you say?

GEORGE You haven't told me who he is.

PAUL Freddy MacLeod, he said.

GEORGE A colleague of sorts. No, that's fine by me. Mind you, I have to admit we have never been exactly friends. Why would he want to look me up under present circumstances, I wonder.

PAUL He said he heard that you and Norma have taken a sabbatical from each other. So will I ring him back and say yes?

GEORGE Of course it's mostly up to you, Paul. They would be your guests. As for me, I think I'm comfortable enough with that.
(PAUL leaves and comes back)

PAUL Ten minutes, he said. He called his friend Carla.

GEORGE	Haven't met her. – I never gave you the details of how Tim was killed, did I. I might be able to talk about it now. Would you mind?
PAUL	Ach no, it's a privilege, George.
GEORGE	I had decided to go to the gym to spite Norma and because I had the car, I picked up the youngsters from school first and took them with me. They were appalled of course, especially Susan, at the prospect of having to spend two hours at the Gym. Suddenly Freddy turns up and wants to sell me something. I say maybe, but first he has to take Timmy and Susan home. I could tell at the time that Susan was planning something but I was glad to be rid of the youngsters – oh God! – yes, I was glad to be rid of them, I was in a rage, Paul. For a split second it occurred to me that I should take them home myself but my hatred of Norma got in the way again and I acted accordingly. And for some reason I can't even feel guilty about it. That worries me.
	(the doorbell – PAUL goes to open; FRED and CARLA enter)
PAUL	Welcome! Welcome! Imagine! Out of the blue. I'm Paul. Can't explain why we've never met. And I recognize *you* right away as Carla because Fred told me on the telephone he would bring someone called Carla. Clever of me, isn't it? How do you do. George, your friend has arrived and brought his own friend, as promised.
GEORGE	Hello Freddy. Carla.
FRED	George! I heard. I think you're doing the right thing.
PAUL	Let's sit down, everybody, why don't we.

42

CARLA	Thank you, Paul, but you know, these two have a lot to talk about. Why don't you and I just leave them to it for a minute. Maybe we can go to your little kitchen there and make some coffee or something. Would you mind awfully?
PAUL	No. Of course.
	(CARLA takes PAUL aside)
GEORGE	I couldn't take it any more, Freddy. Paul rescued me. I think I'm still numb since Timmy died. Even looking at Norma gave me the shivers. But how are you coping?
FRED	You might say that I've been rescued too. Carla's a natural. When she talks I feel easy. Doesn't it seem strange, how you and I have had our heads knocked together. I'm finally able to sleep a little at night.
GEORGE	Yes, that's still a problem for me. It's terrifying, when you realize that you're a stranger to yourself. I think I've only half lived until now. My own children, my wife, they have meant nothing to me, Freddy. Nothing.
FRED	How amazing that you should be able to realize that now!
GEORGE	I do. I do realize it.
FRED	And for me, it seems to be more of a case of coming to terms with the fact that I don't amount to anything. I said that to Carla. I said: I'm a mere thing, Carla, have nothing to do with me. And do you know what she said to me? She said: Think about me instead for a while. That will fix you.
GEORGE	She said that?

FRED	She did. And I've started on that process of … of resurrection. Believe it or not, I am actually making a point of that – of thinking more about Carla than about myself. After Timmy it was downhill. It felt like the bottom had finally been knocked out of me. Think about it. A child *you* never cared about, a child *I* had barely got to know, dies under circumstances that could be ascribed almost entirely to the realm of the accidental – with far-reaching effects. – What do you think, should we invite Carla and George to join us again? That was sensitive of Carla, wasn't it.
GEORGE	Yes. That's good. I feel fine about that now. Talking about it. I'll call them. *(GEORGE brings PAUL and CARLA* *in from the kitchen)* Carla, I was grateful for that little chat with George, under four eyes, as it were.
CARLA	Yes, I thought that might do you good. Paul and I talked about what happened. And we agreed that it's important.
FRED	I remember you said: Now you have to make it work for you – or words to that effect and I first thought: Whatever is she talking about? Then gradually it began to make sense. We're here for one another, not for getting choked up in our problems.
GEORGE	And Paul has saved *my* bacon. He just plucked me out of the mess I was creating with Norma. I was literally incapable of doing anything useful for myself.
CARLA	What about Norma, George? How is she coping?
GEORGE	Carla, I can't bear thinking about that yet. We're not in touch. She's in Crete with Henry's friend Irma.

CARLA	And who is Henry?
GEORGE	Henry is married to Phillipa, who in turn is a friend of Norma's.
CARLA	So Irma, Henry's friend, is in Crete with George's wife? That's beautiful! Life is truly stranger than fiction.
FRED	And you know how to take advantage of that, don't you, Carla.
CARLA	Well, I look at it this way. We wander from A to B and from B to C with never a care in the world when suddenly the roof falls in and buries us up to the neck in rubble. Then we start to dig one another out. Not ourselves but one another. That's where I come in. I think I was literally born to point out to people that individual independence and private emotions are about as useless as their opposites. So when I bumped into Fred here I realized I had my work cut out for me.
FRED	Believe me, I will do all I can to cooperate.
GEORGE	So when you advised Fred to care for you instead for himself, that was literally a selfless suggestion?
CARLA	Not so much selfless as practical and useful, George. A lot of our hang-ups sort *themselves* out when we forget about ourselves, and there's only one way to forget about ourselves, and that is by concentrating on the welfare of someone else. So would you call that being selfless?
GEORGE	Nor really. I see what you mean. So Paul, did you realize you were doing yourself some good when you decided to do *me* a favour?
PAUL	I did after a while, yes. At first, I dare say, it was a generous impulse. More than generous, really. I

45

believe we're talking about community here. More specifically communality. My belief, as I work it out day by day these days, is developing in the following direction: We are endowed, from birth, with a fundamental, human-natural instinct for community and it works spontaneously. If morality has anything going for it, then it leads us to the realization of that instinct and thereafter we can forget about morality.

FRED   Morality as a crutch. Religion as a crutch. I get it.

CARLA   If you've ever had a broken leg, you're grateful for a crutch.

PAUL   And as modern individuals, don't we all have broken legs?

GEORGE   As modern individuals, yes. That's good. But, according to you, or rather according to you janitor friend Jimmy, not as contemporary persons.

CARLA   Yes, that's when we communicate, right?

FRED   Which is what we're doing at the moment. I love it.

PAUL   And if we were to do it exclusively for our little group here we would soon run into problems again. A group slides as readily into egotism as an individual.

GEORGE   As a society, right? A church? A nation state?

FRED   That's interesting. So the four of us have to keep in mind that we're performing actors, who do what we do for an audience.

CARLA   I agree completely with that. As soon as we enclose ourselves in four walls we die.

PAUL   And when we choose to die rather than live, we automatically invite others to follow in our footsteps.

FRED	So even conversation has to be open-ended, right?
CARLA	Which reminds me, I have a hair-dresser's appointment. She comes to my house in the evening and does my hair much better than I can for a fiver, and believe me, she needs the money more than I do.
PAUL	Right! So we say good-bye and my guess is we will meet again soon.
GEORGE	A very good idea! Carla, it's been a special pleasure meeting you. I'm happy for you too, Freddy. Hold on to that one. She's a keeper.
CARLA	Ah, now, there's a whole different conversation we can have about that some day. About keeping and holding and clinging and possessing.
GEORGE	True enough, it makes me nervous even hearing those words mentioned all in a row.
FRED	Like links in a chain, right?

(freeze)

―――

14

(NORMA and IRMA in an apartment in Crete)

NORMA	I can't very well sit on the beach and roast in the sun all day, Irma. I need to find something interesting to do. Also, I'm tired of reading this stupid book. Who has ever heard of this writer anyway! I'm an intelligent woman and I need my challenges.
IRMA	This is only our second day. Try to keep in mind why we came here.

NORMA	Refresh my memory, dear?
IRMA	Do you know what, Norma? You are an obnoxious individual and a sentimental one rolled into one. Now don't forget that I'm stronger than you are, so I won't stand for any violence. I admit I may well have taken on more than I can handle but I'm not through trying yet. Please notice, I'm smiling.
NORMA	Oh Irma, don't go sour on me, please. You're my last hope.
IRMA	You do realize that you've been getting away with murder. – And so has your husband. You are two of a kind, except that he is weak and you are violent. It amounts to the same. I imagined that by separating you two, you might come to see himself in the round. You notice how I'm perfectly at ease and at peace while I say all this to you.
NORMA	You should yell at me. Put me in my place. Curse me for a stupid bitch. I would understand that.
IRMA	Ah, but that is the stupid bitch half of you talking. When you start whining, poor you, misunderstood, please help me – that's the other half. What I'm trying to help you with is the person in the middle. Are you not able to look me in the eye and tell me that sometimes you actually love?
NORMA	When do I love? You tell me.
IRMA	Not when you feel like it but when you decide to love?
NORMA	And why would I decided to love?
IRMA	Because it's the only powerful solution to the problem of a disturbed psyche, whether it's mine or yours.

NORMA	Oh very well. I'm tired of arguing. Just to please you, I shall love.
IRMA	Start with George.
NORMA	No. Don't ask me to do that. Too much hate has accumulated.
IRMA	Alright, love *me* then. I'm close at hand and you won't have much of a build-up of resentment and contempt to overcome.
NORMA	A revolting suggestion but I'll try.
IRMA	Excellent. Are you doing it now?
NORMA	It feels like nothing.
IRMA	Good. It's not meant to.
NORMA	You're really asking me to behave like a youngster, aren't you.
IRMA	Probably youngsters, if they love, do it without thinking. I'm asking you to think at the same time. Know what you're doing while you're doing it. Know that you love while you love.
NORMA	What do you suppose it is that makes us go all psychic?
IRMA	The fact that for too long we don't love.
NORMA	And I don't even have to like you to love you, isn't that right?
IRMA	Hey, why don't you find out for yourself?
NORMA	Well, I don't like you at all at the moment because you don't tell me what I want to hear. So it seems that in order to love you, all I have to do is get rid of that dislike first and then …

IRMA	No no, Norma. Just go ahead and love. Love is powerful and crowds those enemy opinions and feelings out of the way. – There. I've told you all you should need to know. Don't be impatient now. Experiment with what works and what doesn't work. I'm going for a walk along the beach. No, I want to go by myself. I have a feeling that my whole approach to this might be wrong. We might just end up going back home with nothing achieved. That would thoroughly confuse me. I would have to rethink a whole lot of things. I'll be back within half an hour.
NORMA	Don't forget your hat.
IRMA	Well … thank you! (*IRMA leaves*)

(lengthy pause)

NORMA	I wonder if this is a madness in me. I wonder if now and again I enjoy getting so angry that it puts my head away. I wonder, if that were the case, is there a good reason for it that has nothing to do with accusation, guilt, blame, judgment. What if there is a chance for me to figure out what is the good reason for me to become so self-righteously hateful at times. I have half an hour to think about this. What if it were in fact up to me to judge, even though no one else in the world wants to be judged. What if it were to turn out that I actually do very poorly what is in fact, from birth, up to me to do? I say 'from birth' because I have always been like this. I have always been – now and again – a thorn in everybody's side. When I notice it, and I see them complain, I become furious because they do not accept what is good for them. Might it in fact be good for them that I judge them? Irma has given me the opportunity to think for myself the thoughts I would never say to anybody. – Actually

I think it's me who is initially being judged. I refuse that judgement and I do it by judging others. I judge others so that I won't be judged. That might be closer to the truth. What if it were good for me to judge and be judged. If I could believe that, I might be able to come to some rest within myself. Possibly it *has* to be believed, in *addition* to being understood. I'm experimenting now, which is what Norma suggested. How could I judge others without them being upset? No, that's weak. If judgement is true it's – bound to – hurt – unless it's done – mercifully? Well, thank you for that – whoever suggested that to me. I certainly didn't come up with it myself. Let merciful judgement be, first of all, what I believe to be a possibility. It would mean judgment without blame. Judgement combined with forgiveness? Difficult. What about judgement combined with humility and forgiveness. A tall order? It works as I think about it – and as I think it through. Merciful judgement – judgement combined with forgiveness and humility. If I could learn that. Oh if I could learn that! Really I'm done with being hateful. It's not that much fun any more. As it turns out, that might not mean necessarily turning into a hypocritical wimp. It might not mean being untrue to myself. Maybe that's why I persecute George, because I'm reluctant to be untrue to myself. Maybe he's not weak at all but merely human and therefore practically unable to cope with – with whatever is the opposite of merciful judgement, which would be – heartless judgment? Criticism? Oh yes, dear me. Is it high time I learned humility and forgiveness? In other words, mercy? I dare say it has taken me so to come round to it because it's especially important for me. So I've become attached to heartless judgment. To self-righteous criticism. God help me, that explains all that sheer misery.

IRMA	(*enters*) I'm back.
NORMA	Oh, I say, was that half an hour?
IRMA	Not quite, but it's hot out there. How are you getting on?
NORMA	I have been thinking, Irma, but ... I don't want to talk about it yet. Can you understand that?
IRMA	Of course I can. I meant to tell you something, even before I went for my walk but I forgot. When I fist met you, at Paul's place, my heart went out to you. I could see only the pain you were in. I suppose that is my strength. I tend to relate to pain and suffering in someone. On the way here, on the plane and on the bus to Hersonnisos, I discovered to my consternation that you were susceptible neither to empathy nor to sympathy. I confess it was a bit of a shock to me. It seemed to me you were full of contempt. I had never met anyone like that. So I decided to behave the way I have behaved during our time in Crete so far. It was new territory for me. Never before in my life would it have occurred to me to speak to someone in the imperative voice. I want you to know that I'm going to stop that now. I don't think I'm doing you much good, Norma, that's the long and the short of it. Let's just try to enjoy ourselves for the rest of our stay here as best we can.
NORMA	(*reaches for her hands*) Irma, I have made headway. Even heartway. Probably both. Fear not for the good effect you've had on me. I think I've made contact with my soul. All my life I have loathed myself for not being kind to people while at the

same time I was full of contempt for the people who could not like me. Your effect on me has been marvellous – probably because you are naturally genuine and sincere. Only listen to the way I talk now. Is that not a change? I don't feel threatened by you and I don't feel anxious in myself. However, I know, there are a million parts of me that need to wake up. You've been a true friend to me even while I didn't like you. I admire you now. I want you to know that. I believe that soon I will be able to show who I really am – not the ...

IRMA   Norma, stop. Don't go on. I am so happy I could weep. I know exactly where you are coming from because I think I have been there, in my own way. This is a marvellous surprise. What say we go for a drive, maybe up to the Lasithi Plateau, there's plenty of time, the sun doesn't set until eight o'clock.

NORMA   And when we get back I'll write a short letter to George. I feel fine about George. We will probably be back home long before the letter arrives but it will do me good to write it.

IRMA   Come. Two bottles of water is all we need.
             (*both leave*)

                              * * * * *